THE FOX AND THE GOOSE

by Mick Gowar and John Joven

W
FRANKLIN WATTS
LONDON•SYDNEY

Long, long ago, all animals were friends.

Animals could talk to each other.

Dogs talked to cats – politely.

Lions and goats spoke to each other – politely.

No animal growled at, or barked at, or bit another animal, and no animal ever ate any other animal. That was the rule.

Fox and Goose lived next door to each other.

They were good neighbours.

In those days, all animals were good neighbours.

That was the rule.

Fox and Goose tried to be friends,
but it wasn't easy. Fox liked to howl
at night, which kept Goose awake.

Goose liked to sing in the morning, which woke up Fox.

"Fox and I should be friends," thought Goose,

"even if he does howl all night."

All animals were supposed to be good friends.

That was the rule.

"I know! I'll do something kind for him.

I'll invite him to dinner."

6

So Goose cooked

a delicious vegetable soup

for them to share.

Goose served the soup

in her two best jugs.

"Yum! Yum!" said Goose.

She could stick her beak into her jug

to finish all her soup.

But Fox couldn't get his snout into his jug.

Fox was angry. "First, Goose sings

in the morning and wakes me up.

Now she cooks a meal that I can't eat.

I do not like Goose!"

"Don't you want your soup?"

asked Goose, surprised.

"No," said Fox crossly.

"I'll have it!" said Goose. "Yum! Yum!"

She put her beak into the jug

and finished all of Fox's soup.

"Now you must invite me to dinner

at your house," said Goose,

wiping her beak. "That is the rule."

Fox was cross with Goose.

He couldn't eat from a jug.

"Goose tried to make me look foolish,"
he thought.

So he decided to get his own back.

He cooked a delicious, thick porridge.

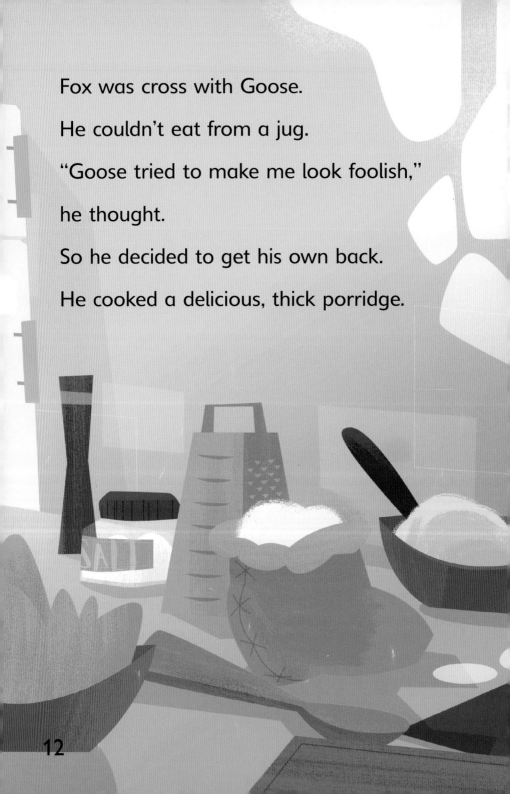

13

Fox served the porridge

on his best dishes.

"Yum! Yum!" said Fox,

and he gobbled up

all his porridge.

Goose tried and tried, but she couldn't eat her porridge from a flat dish.

Goose was angry. "First, Fox howls all night and keeps me awake. Now he cooks a meal I can't eat. I do not like Fox."

"Don't you want your porridge?"
asked Fox.

"No," said Goose crossly.

"I'll have it!" said Fox.
And he gobbled up
all Goose's porridge.

16

So, Goose was cross with Fox because
she couldn't eat from a dish.
And Fox was cross with Goose because
he couldn't eat from a jug.
They forgot the rule that
all animals should be friends.
Some animals said
Goose was right.
Some animals said
Fox was right.

There were big fights. No one could agree.
Soon all the animals forgot the rule that
all animals should be friends.
So now dogs chase cats and lions chase deer.
Foxes chase geese and geese are afraid of foxes
– and all because they couldn't be kind
to each other. Isn't that a shame?

Story order

Look at these 5 pictures and captions.
Put the pictures in the right order
to retell the story.

1

Fox made dinner for Goose.

2

All the animals had a fight.

3

Goose could not eat from a dish.

4

Goose made dinner for Fox.

5

Fox could not eat from a jug.

Independent Reading

This series is designed to provide an opportunity for your child to read on their own. These notes are written for you to help your child choose a book and to read it independently.

In school, your child's teacher will often be using reading books which have been banded to support the process of learning to read. Use the book band colour your child is reading in school to help you make a good choice. *The Fox and the Goose* is a good choice for children reading at Gold Band in their classroom to read independently.

The aim of independent reading is to read this book with ease, so that your child enjoys the story and relates it to their own experiences.

About the book

In this retelling of an Aesop fable, we meet Fox and Goose, at a time when all animals were friends. They invite each other to dinner, but their lack of understanding for each other's needs causes a huge argument between them.

Before reading

Help your child to learn how to make good choices by asking: "Why did you choose this book? Why do you think you will enjoy it?" Look at the cover together and ask: "What do you think the story will be about?" Ask your child to think of what they already know about fox and geese. Then ask your child to read the title aloud. Ask: "Do you think that foxes and geese are usually friends?" Remind your child that they can sound out the letters to make a word if they get stuck. Decide together whether your child will read the story independently or read it aloud to you.

During reading

Remind your child of what they know and what they can do independently. If reading aloud, support your child if they hesitate or ask for help by telling the word. If reading to themselves, remind your child that they can come and ask for your help if stuck.

After reading

Support comprehension by asking your child to tell you about the story. Use the story order puzzle to encourage your child to retell the story in the right sequence, in their own words. The correct sequence can be found on the next page.

Help your child think about the messages in the book that go beyond the story and ask: "Why do you think Fox and Goose fell out? Could they have tried to understand each other better? How could the other animals have helped them? What did they do instead?"

Give your child a chance to respond to the story: "Have you ever upset anybody by accident? Have you ever been involved in an argument between friends? What do you think is the best way to end an argument?"

Extending learning

Help your child predict other possible outcomes of the story by asking: "If Fox had explained the problem to Goose in the first place, what do you think might have happened? Do you think they would have still had an argument?"

In the classroom, your child's teacher may be teaching different kinds of sentences. There are many examples in this book that you could look at with your child, including statements, exclamations and questions. Find these together and point out how the end punctuation can help us decide what kind of sentence it is.

Franklin Watts
First published in Great Britain in 2020
by The Watts Publishing Group

Series Editors: Jackie Hamley and Melanie Palmer
Series Advisors: Dr Sue Bodman and Glen Franklin
Series Designers: Peter Scoulding and Cathryn Gilbert

A CIP catalogue record for this book is
available from the British Library.

ISBN 978 1 4451 7179 1 (hbk)
ISBN 978 1 4451 7180 7 (pbk)
ISBN 978 1 4451 7313 9 (library ebook)

Printed in China

Franklin Watts
An imprint of
Hachette Children's Group
Part of The Watts Publishing Group
Carmelite House
50 Victoria Embankment
London EC4Y 0DZ

An Hachette UK Company
www.hachette.co.uk

www.reading-champion.co.uk

Answer to Story order: 4, 5, 1, 3, 2